THIS BOOK BELONGS TO:

The cover of this book has been designed using resources from freepik.com
image: fruits-stickers_23-2147510219

Ordering Information:
Special discounts are available on large quantity purchases by not-for-profit organizations, associations, and others.

For details contact:
Cuzzos Publishing and Media at cuzzospublishingandmedia@gmail.com
Orders by U.S. trade bookstores and wholesalers can contact the same email above.
First Edition, First Printing, 2020

Special Thanks: Thank you to all the friends and family who helped bring this book to life.
We could not have done this without your comments, ideas, critiques and continued support!

If you made it all the way to this line, thank you for taking the time to read all this stuff and support this book!
We hope you get the message. You have value. You are valued. Find your purpose. Now get to reading please!
Hank Huckleberry needs your help!

When Good Fruit Goes Bad

Written and Illustrated by Vernon D. Gibbs II and Steven T. Gray

A CUZZOS BOOK

Hank Huckleberry woke up early every single day, and started every morning in exactly the same way.

He brushed his teeth

and showered.

then dried off and checked his hair, but didn't brush because he didn't have too much up there.

He checked the mirror to make sure that his moustache was neat, and then he went down to the kitchen for something to eat.

"Good morning, here's your daily apple," his wife Cindy said.
Hank ate an apple every day: juicy, shiny and red.

"No, thank you my dear I think that this apple's day has passed.
It's bruised and looks a little dry and should go in the trash."

He skipped his daily apple, but he had some toast and juice.
He ate and read his paper then said, "Time to sell some fruit!"

When Hank opened his fruit store, cherries flew right past his head.
And what he saw then made him wish that he had stayed in bed.

The apples were upset because they were no longer fresh.
They fought with dented oranges and made a fruity mess!

A bunch of grapes were trying to hide from the fighting fruits, afraid they'd get caught in the battle and squished into juice.

The grapefruits that were always bitter, now they had a reason.
They were soft and spotty and would soon be out of season.

Bananas, over ripe and mushy, laughed as poor Hank slipped,
into an awkward and very funny banana split.

The smaller fruits like grapes and cherries had no fun at all.
The larger fruits kicked them around like they were soccer balls.

Hank's customers bought his fresh fruit so fast he never had a chance to open up his store and see good fruit go bad.

His fruit were always good and fresh, Hank sold only the best. What would his customers think now if they could see this mess?

He had to stop and think and try to come up with a plan...

...and FAST because the fruit were swinging from the ceiling fan!

He called his good friend Sarah Sweets,
"Miss Sweets, what should I do?"

"My fruits are bad and no one knows
more about fruit than you!"

She showed up lighting fast! Bad pears and apples on the shelves were thumping some good plums when she yelled, " STOP! Explain yourselves!"

The leader of the bad fruit stood up with something to say.
To Hank's surprise it was the apple his wife threw away.

The angry apple yelled "Hear this, I speak for all bad fruits!
We're sick of being tossed if we're not perfect, round or cute."

"We get left out on counter tops or stuffed into the fridge.
If we're not perfect, we get thrown right into the garbage!"

"We might not be the freshest fruit but we can still be used.
You're picky and so quick to throw us out because we're bruised!"

Miss Sweets came closer so she could talk to the angry fruit.
"Now wait one second Mr. Apple, that's not the whole truth.

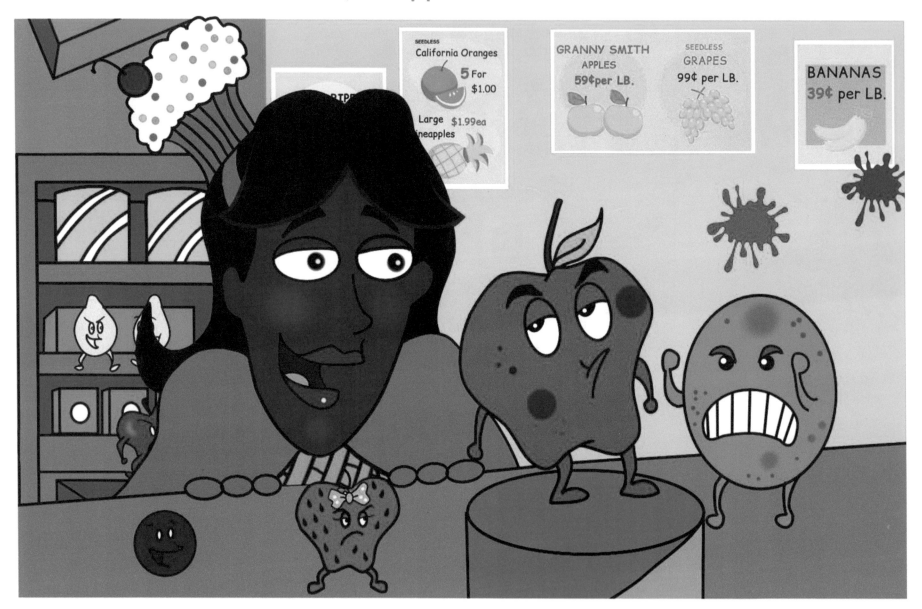

Some people throw good fruit away you are perfectly right.
Maybe it's that they think you're bad when you're just overripe."

"Let's show them how you can be saved if you're up to the task.
How can this bad fruit still be good? Well I'm so glad you asked!

I save overripe fruit, I don't just let them go to waste.
They may be bruised or oddly shaped, but still have lots of taste."

"They're sweet, and full of fiber, full of vitamins and more.
I know some yummy food and drinks that you can be used for.

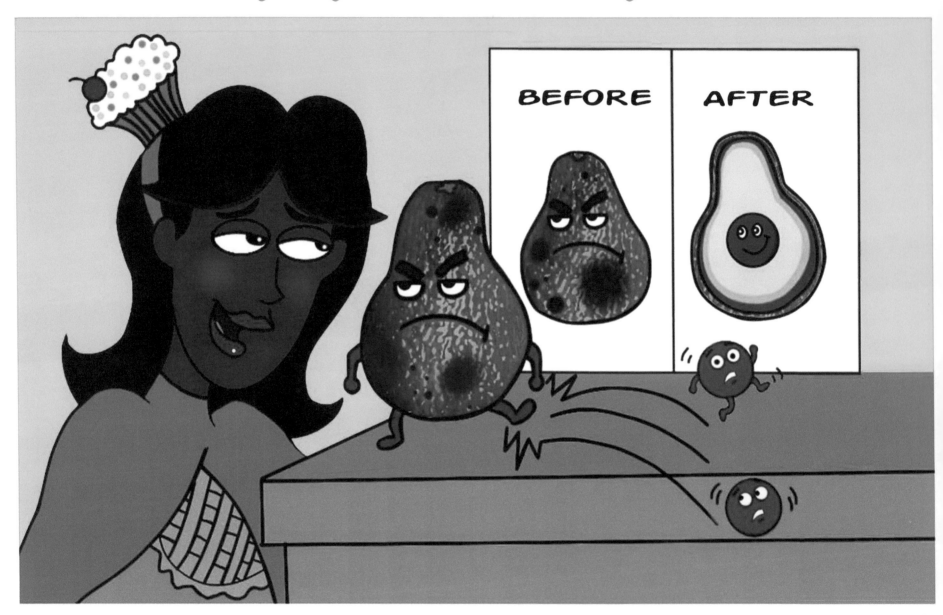

I see you angry avocado, but please don't be mean.
You still make guacamole that's tasty, healthy and green."

"Speckled bananas are still great so why don't you instead,
stop fighting and become some delicious banana bread?

You problem peaches can be used as well, you're not alone.
You'll make amazing muffins, a peach cobbler or some scones."

"Blueberry, blackberry, raspberry and strawberry fans,
even when mushy, berries make tasty jellies and jams."

"And, Mr. Apple, I haven't forgotten you of course.
Imperfect, though you still can make the perfect applesauce.

Some apples can be damaged but still candied, baked or dried.
Soft, sweet or tart, you're the best part of good old apple pie."

What Miss Sweets said made them feel better and they all agreed.
Fruit can be used, freshly picked or bruised, including the seeds.

Of course we should throw fruits away if they're spoiled or rotten.
Fruits, when bruised may still be used, don't let that be forgotten.

Hank agreed with Sarah Sweets to not waste fruit again.
"Veggies go bad," said Mr. Apple, "keep an eye on them!"

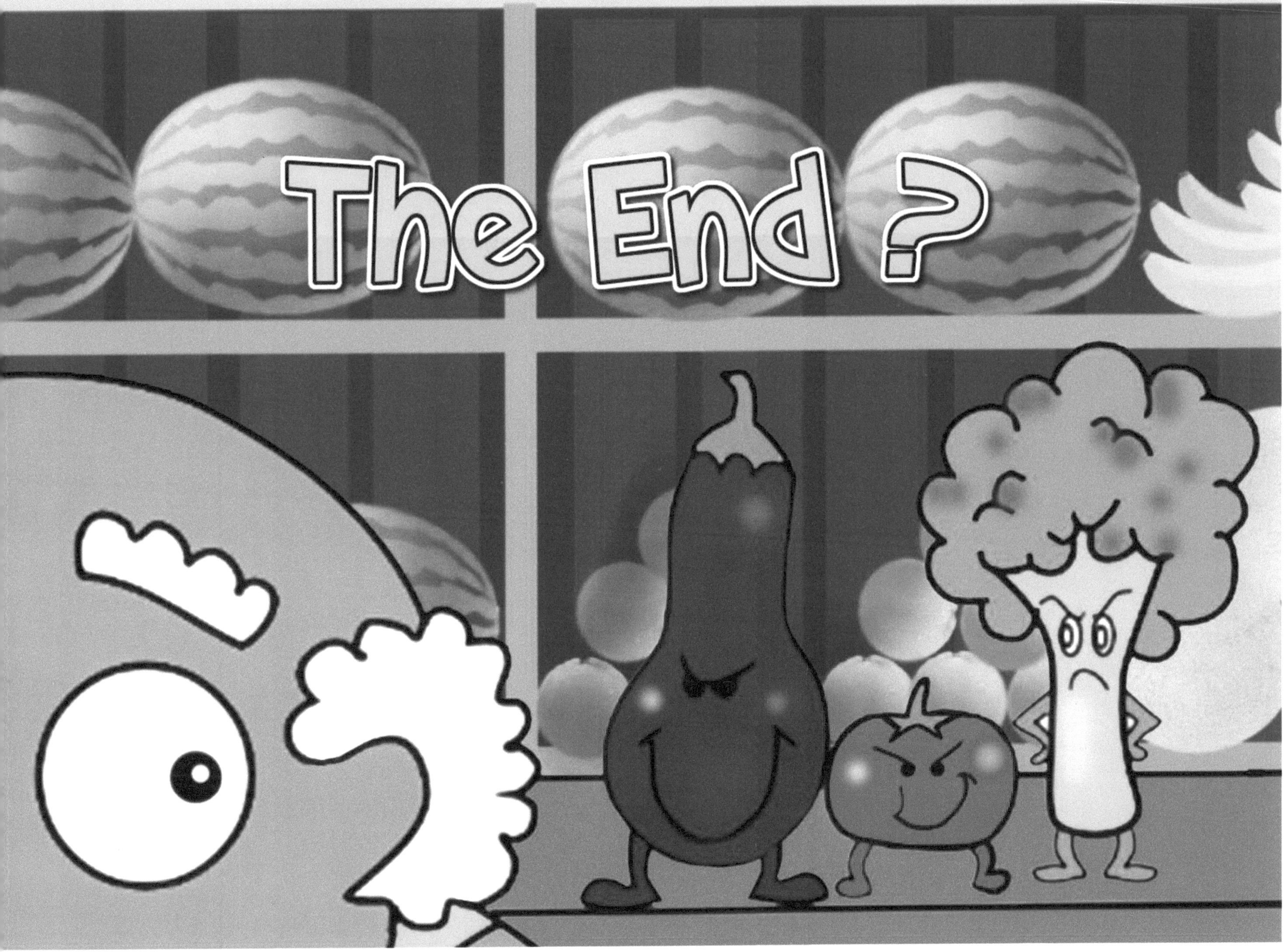
The End ?

CPSIA information can be obtained
at www.ICGtesting.com
Printed in the USA
BVHW050515210322
631473BV00001B/1